Cutting the Cord

Unleashing A Mothers Prayers

Marilyn Kay Brooks Simmons

This book is dedicated to my three children, whom I love dearly with everything in me. I pray and hope that they see me as the best mother ever. If that is a goal that I've attained, then I am at peace. Though there have been many mistakes and lots of trial and error, neither one of you ever made me feel inadequate. I pray that you all will be blessed with children as wonderful as each of you has been to me. I am blessed to say that it is my great joy to see that you all did not fall once I cut the cord but rose high above as eagles. I love you all for life: Akayla Cha'Nell, Keara Shantell, and Keith Morris. Forever My Babies!!!!

Truly my prayers have been unleashed.

Acknowledgments

First, I gladly bow my knees, giving all glory and honor to God for blessing me with the gift of writing. This book came as an inspiration from God to me word for word, and I thank Him for it. All praise to God for how helpful this book has been to me and will be to others.

To my husband, James Simmons Jr., thank you for believing in me and encouraging me to soar beyond what I ever dreamed. I love you: Til toe Tag, Sir.

To my children. Thank you, Akayla, Keara, and Keith, for letting me love you all and for being so loving even when the cord was tight on you all. I love you all. To my grandchild Lauryn Kay, GiGi loves you, and thanks to you for giving her a whole new type of love.

To my two one and onlies Carolyn and Lee Brooks, I love you all. Thanks, Stephanie Brooks Perkins, for the memory of me always choosing writing over playing as a small child.

To QuiNina J. Sinceno and GDI Publishing, thanks for making another dream come true. To all my family and friends, I love you all dearly.

Introduction

Train up a child in the way he should go, and when he is old, he will not depart from it.

Proverbs 22:6

Hello, and welcome to the beauty of God's blessing. In the midst of me going forth and doing what I do daily, God spoke to me and said… "There is more."

I have a talk show that God had given me called "A Touch of Seasoning," On a particular Saturday, I was supposed to speak on the topic Cutting the Cord. Well, the first Saturday, it was postponed because I was on an anniversary trip with my husband. The following Saturday, a winter storm had hit Texas and left us without power and water. Therefore, I still had not done this segment before I began to write this book. I did the segment with a newfound appreciation for God.

I also have a book club that I created. Well, we were reading a book about praying for our husbands at this particular time. I also have a book on praying with authority and praying for your wife and several books about how to pray and whom to pray for.

God showed me that we have several books out about praying for ourselves, our ministry, and our husbands, but nothing out there is centered on praying for our children. So, this is where the message "There is more" comes in.

I had my heart set on doing something with the book club's women, and I am at a place where I need to cut the cord and release my children to God.

My son will soon be eighteen, and my two daughters are in their early twenties; one is a mother now as well. I can admit that I have a tight grip on the cords of motherhood, which has stressed me out to the max.

God is speaking to me in this book, and I know that He is speaking to all mothers as well. This is not going to be an easy read, but it will be a life-changing one.

I will be including prayers that God has given me specifically and prayers that others have inspired or contributed. So, dive in and get all these golden nuggets. I'm trying to help a mom, dad, and child today; yes, even one will bless my soul.

After you purchase and read this book, I request that you send me a short email or messenger to let me know how it impacted your life and future. I will be sure and leave this information at the end of this book.

Preface

What does it mean to cut something? It is the separation or opening of a physical object, into two or more portions, through the application of an acutely directed force.

Wow!!!! This definition alone gives me chills because it sums my book up in a manner that is only God.

Let me break this down for you all so that you all get it. First, separation. Mothers, this is a word that seems to give us a gut punch when it comes to our children. It is one of the hardest things for us to contemplate.

Even when we are pregnant and at that ninth month when giving birth and separate physically from our babies, that is a hard, painful process. We scream, we cry, and we call on God.

However, in the end, there is such a beautiful blessing that we have before us. The moment the cord has been cut, we get to walk into a whole other wonderful era of our lives; motherhood.

So, we have to look at the cutting as a beautiful and wonderful blessing that we get to walk into and not a bad thing

When the cord is cut at birth, it is not done by us because we are not in a position to be able to do so; we are not qualified to do the cutting.

Well, as our children grow up, God allows us different tests and lessons along the way to train and qualify us to be able to cut the cord. When they are at a place where they no longer need to be connected to us on every level when they are no longer totally dependent on us for food, shelter, water, advice, protection, money, comfort, provisions, hugs, and support, it is hard for us to let go. Yet, we have been prepared all along to do so.

As mothers, we play many roles, and at this point, we have to be the surgeon who picks up the tool and cuts the cord.

Once we cut that cord, God then becomes the Father to that child. All their burdens, needs, desires, and hearts' content is in His hands.

Understanding that this is the absolute best place for them to be will unleash a prayer in us that is complete.

Therefore, the cutting may seem like a heart-wrenching task; it is for the greater good of our children, their future, and their eternity in Christ.

The second word I want to hone in on is opening. When we open a door, someone goes out, and someone comes in. When we open our minds, wisdom goes out, and wisdom comes in. When we open our hearts, love goes out, and love comes in. These are not the only words that could fill in these spaces, but God's positive words had me fill in the spaces with.

It shows that when you open your life to God, He can come in and fill it with all the love, positivity, wisdom, and provisions that we need. He does that for us, and He will do that for our children as well if we open up.

The next thing I want to focus on is the two or more portions part of the definition.

We have to realize that our children are complex. Not only are they our children, but they are their own individual persons, and they are people who belong to God. They may be mothers, fathers, teachers, best friends, counselors, husbands, wives, prayer warriors. They are not just one part. They do not belong only to us.

This makes it a lot easier for us to let them go when we realize that they are not just ours.

Finally, I wanted to talk about the direct force.

This tells me that God is accurate, He is in control, and He is a force. When He tells us to let go, it is in our best interest to do just that. It is never a good thing to buck against what God is doing.

He is our creator, and He is the most powerful and omnipotent force there has ever been and will ever be. We can rest assured that when we cut the cord and unleash our prayers unto Him, He hears us and that our children are in the best of hands.

Table of Contents

Chapter One

Our Father

First, as I write this book, I am forced to look back on my childhood and face where the entanglement of my own cord comes into play. I was my mother's third and final child...that most people knew of. I later came to realize that, in fact, I was not just the third and last child. I was not just the baby that my mother was smothering and not giving any space. I was not just the teenager who was so stifled and restricted by an invisible cord.

My mother had previously miscarried three or four (I am not definite on the number) babies. I was her rainbow baby. I was her miracle child. I was the one that made it. I was the one God saw fit to come into this world and do what He had instilled in me to do before I was ever formed in her womb.

I sometimes look back on my life and wonder if I knew this, would I had been a lot quicker to walk in my purpose? Would I have been a better mother from day one?

I had to stop holding myself captive to the what-ifs. For, if I had known, I might have deemed myself unique or regal and wanted to take credit for something that only God deserved such credit. It was His plan, and it had nothing to do with me. There is nothing that I can go back and change with my childhood or how I raised my children. However, I can now embark upon a new journey to help other mothers to cut the cord. This book is intended to show mothers that they will not always get it exactly right, but they can always lean on God to do things righteously and that no, they will not be perfect parents, but that they have the one who makes all things ideal living on the inside.

The goal here is to not beat yourself up for generational curses that have kept you bound and lost. Those curses that we will deal with in later chapters have to be broken from your mind and heart to succeed at parenting/raising healthy, loving, and secure children. Children who know to depend on God before their mom. I know that sounds crazy, but they have to learn where their help comes from at an early age.

I did not learn much, and I was so broken and lost when my mom died. I was a grown woman with three kids, yet all my hope was in my mother, not God.

What a dangerous position to be in. Let us not find ourselves putting our children in such a predicament. Let us give them the tools, the mindset, the word, and the power to know that it is God over everything and everyone.

We know that all these ties our children get wrapped up in are nothing more than satanic schemes and plots to kill them. He does not want them to rise up and be that strong force against him and his kingdom. He desires to steal, kill, and destroy them. We have to wage war on satan as parents that it stops here.

We have to understand that as much as we love our children, the best thing we can do, especially once they reach a certain age, is to cut the cord.

Holding on to them as they try to grow and feel their way through life is only a hindrance to them and us as parents. We are so used to nurturing that we do not know how and when to stop nurturing and release them back to God.

It is my prayer that we all see ourselves in this book and break the ties that bind. The enemy created those ties.

God created the bond between a mother and child, and He never meant for that bond to turn into bondage. Now that is deep. However, we all know that every single thing that God creates, the enemy reaches his grubby, dirty hands in and tries to imitate. We have to be steadfast in our prayers for our children. Still, before we can do that, again, we must delve into our own past and upbringing to break cycles of negativity, wrong thinking, and generational curses. We can no longer raise our kids in family tradition, or like granny and

Meemaw used to. It is time for us to step outside of the box and cut the cord.

Before moving any further with praying for our kids, I want our first prayer to be to our Father for us, His children. Please pray this prayer with me and believe God to release you from anything that binds you or that will re-tie or recreate invisible cords. Cords that we often do not want to admit are there, still dangling and holding on for dear life, all the while causing death.

Prayer: Our Father

Dear Heavenly Father, first, I thank you for being my Father. Thank you for being my example of everything good and perfect in your sight. Thank you for blessing me to have such unique and beautiful creatures you call children, which you gave to me. I am so in awe of you. God, I ask that you will forgive me for the times I did not appreciate you as a Father, the times that I did not appreciate my mother as a mother. I know that she did not have all the answers, but even in that, she did not have you in her heart. I forgive her for all the wrong decisions and all the wrong information. I release myself from the past of whatever I felt she did that held me back. It was nothing but love and good intentions on her part, and for that, I am grateful. I thank you that amid all ignorance and misguided thoughts and actions that you saved me, you preserved me and that you chose me.

Even if I am that child turned adult reading this whose mother/parent did not know how to love me, did not know how to cherish the gift you gave, I thank you for being that source of love and encouragement. I made it through. I release that parent to you. I am no longer holding on to bitterness, unforgiveness, doubt, feelings of worthlessness. I am enough, despite what deceitful seeds the enemy tried to plant in my head and in my heart. There is no more room for any of that. I belong to you. I have a good Father, and I am enough.

Thank you, God, for breaking those chains, those ties that had me bound, those cords that needed to be cut. I am forgiven; I forgive my mother, father, guardian, whomever that raised me.

I am seeking that forgiveness from my children, and I am seeking to be a Godly mother to them, and I realize that I need you one thousand percent to do that. Lord, please come into my heart, mend it, come into my mind, renew it, come into my life, and resurrect everything.

I am a praying mother, and I am about to be unleashed because I trust in you and because I am free. Thank You, Lord, for this freedom and this declaration.

Strongholds are being broken right now, and I walk in this power and authority now and forevermore. May the children you lent to me come back to you when it is their time saved, sanctified, and holy ghost filled. Knowing without a doubt that they were loved and that they mattered to their mom. Let them see

that she gave them the best gift
ever...You. In Jesus' name, I pray.
Amen.

Chapter Two

Their Minds

Sometimes we project the way we were raised on our kids unconsciously and later recognize when our own children have children, and we see ourselves in them. It is time to cut that cord of generational curses now. We need to be more aware of our words and actions. The way we speak to our children can affect them in a way that is detrimental to their growth, self-esteem, emotional health, mental health, and spiritual well-being.

Too often, we say that sticks and stones may break my bones, but words will never hurt. That is one of the most fabricated statements to date. Words definitely hurt; they tear down and destroy, they steal, and they kill. These are all things that the enemy/satan comes to do. We, as parents, especially saved parents have no place in doing these things.

There is great power in the tongue. It is the smallest member of the body, yet the most powerful, and can be the most potent. That is why God tells us we should be quick to listen and slow to speak. As parents, we often feel that children should be seen and not heard, and in that, we take away their voice all the way spewing out whatever we want to speak. This is not of God. Everyone should have a voice and have that voice respected. We need to learn to talk to our children. We need to open the doors of communication with them. We need to be the parent, the guiding light, the instructor, the first leader that they turn to.

We are to train up a child in the way they should go, and when they are old, they will not depart from it. That way is God's way. We need to not only teach our children about God and the bible, but we need to live it and speak it because there are enough negative influences in the world teaching them sinful ways.

As mothers, fathers, or guardians, we have to guard our words and know that what we as parents say to our children will guide their entire being.

For instance, if a child is loved on at home, told they are valued at home, told they are beautiful at home, told that they are strong at home, told that they are worthy at home, told that they are a warrior at home, told that they are smart at home, told that they are sons and daughters of the king and no weapon formed against them shall prosper, no amount of bullying or negativity can break that belief. It has been instilled in them. We need to be that force.

As a young girl, I had a mom who loved me dearly, with everything in her, and she would hug me and hold me and wipe away my tears every time someone told me I was worthless, that I wasn't pretty enough, that I wasn't smart enough, or that I would never amount to anything. That was all wonderful and much needed, but there was no replacement of words for the tearing down.

See, when something is taken away, it has to be replaced with something else, or the taking away never seems to have occurred.

Spiritually when you preach a powerful sermon, you have given so much of yourself, and you need to be restored; you need to be replenished in the word and in your strength. You need other saints to pray with you; you need to get back to the word; you need to spend more time with God because if not, that which has gone out for others and left you drained can be filled with thoughts, not of God; fleshly desires.

The same goes for when you pray an evil spirit out someone; you do not just pray it out; you must bind that thing, meaning that you forbid it to continue by authority of Jesus Christ. When this is done, that spirit is loosed, but it then goes to and fro seeking a new home. If that has not been replaced with a spirit of holiness, guess what? That same evil spirit will come back to dwell therein.

So, we need to be mindful that when our children are told negative things that we bind those thoughts and lose positivity and peace, blessings, and success into their spirits.

I know that can be hard if we have not grown up that way and if we have not been accustomed to such ways. This is where God comes in. This is where prayer comes in; this is where change comes in; this is where a renewed mind comes in; this is where selflessness comes in. This is where the unleashing of a mother's prayers come in. (When I say mother, fathers, and guardians, you are included)

God wants us to edify with our words. That is why He teaches us to be kind, respectful, civil, loving, and treat others with dignity. Though I am paraphrasing, this is exemplified when God says in I Peter 2:17 to honor all people. Love the brotherhood. Fear God. Honor the king. This proves that everyone deserves respect and love.

In Matthew 25:40, He tells us that whatever we do unto the least of brethren, that we've done unto him. This means that if we love and serve God, we should also love and serve man, those in need, the humble, and those who cannot do for themselves. These are not just good manners, but they are Christian virtues. We are to exhibit and instill such Christian values in our children.

Let us pray for our children now that they know the love of Christ, that they not be bound by tormenting spirits, that they not feel worthless, that they never feel they are alone, and cannot come to us as parents. Let us pray a prayer that forbids satan to have his way with our children. Let us cover their minds.

Prayer: Their minds

Dear Heavenly Father, we come to you in humbleness and reverence. We ask that you teach us to have a spirit of approachability and love when it comes to our children. Father, we are asking you to give us the words to lead and guide them to you. Father, help our children to know that you fearfully and wonderfully made them. God, where the enemy comes in with doubt, fear, lies, deceit, malice, evil, hurtful, and spiteful words, we pray that you would destroy such thoughts and replace them with peace, love, worth, adoration, strength, honor, integrity, and power.

God, we pray that you would touch our children's hearts and break the generational curses that desire to consume them. God, we request that you show them who you created them to be and give them a glimpse into the glorious future ahead of them.

Father, where the enemy tries to plant seeds of hopelessness, we pray that you stir up the gifts in them and allow them to flourish.

God helps us as parents start from day one with a new beginning and a new perspective on what love is and how we should parent, regardless of our past experiences.

God help us to be our children's guiding light to you. For in you all things are good and perfect.

God, touch every child's mind contemplating suicide because they do not feel loved or feel necessary. God replace that lie with your truth and your undying love for them. God cease any thoughts of evil that satan may plant in any child's mind to harm another. God bind the ties and cut the cords that your love, power, and salvation be released right now in the name of Jesus. God, bring forth a new mind, a new creature in not only our children but in us. In Jesus' name, I pray, Amen and Amen.

Chapter Three

Their Hearts

Once we have done all that we can do to encourage and strengthen our children in who they are to us and what they mean to us, it is time to plant holiness in them. This is not the first seed, but believe me, it is the most important. I know that you may feel it should have been first, but for a person to live holy and be strong in the Lord, they first have to be strong, period.

It is not a good idea to send someone onto the battlefield when they have not been trained. The same is with our children. We give them the word of God and nuggets and truths about God always, but as they grow, we go deeper. It is now time to go deeper.

It is a significant loss not being able to grow up in a household of faith. I did not have that blessing. I was the one in my family who decided to go to church and who came to know God for myself. I genuinely wish that I had a solid Christian foundation at home to lead and guide me. I did not. However, God is not slack. He always makes a way.

I came to know God for myself, and I established an amazing relationship with Him; and He has taught me how to be a loving daughter, a patient mother, and an anointed writer. When God was growing me and shaping and molding me, I had no idea that he was laying such a strong foundation for my future. It is so important to know god and to be able to get into that secret place with him. This is not only for yourself but for your children as well.

If you are reading this book, I want you to make sure that you get in a place with God where you are in a relationship with Him so that you can give your children such a foundation.

There will come a time when we have to cut the cord, and it is much easier to do so when you know that you have instilled the word of God in your children. It is much easier to let them go because you know your prayers are at the forefront in the release.

You know that they will be released into the arms of God and not this evil world. That assurance means so much to a parent.

I used to have fear and anxiety about everything my children wanted to do that took them out of my presence. If they wanted to go spend the night with friends, it was usually a no-go; the times that I did say yes, I was continuously calling and checking up on them. I always worried that no one would be able to take care of them the way I could.

This is not to say anything bad about the company they kept because they genuinely were all blessed to have outstanding groups of friends with loving parents. Still, a mother's love is something to contend with.

However, the more I grew in Christ, the more I could relinquish that control and let go, knowing that no one, not even me, Mother, could take better care of them than God.

He was always with them, covering them when I couldn't be there to do so.

Even in that God took away the fear and anxiety, I enjoyed the times when they went away to spend time with friends or other family members. Do not allow the enemy to short-change your happiness by weighing you down with fear.

As soon as your child is born, begin reading the bible to them in some form. It can be through children's books or even stories that you create yourself based on the bible. This way, when they get off the milk and onto the meat of the word, they will be prepared in

their little hearts. Again when you instill greatness in a child, it is hard for anyone to discourage them. It is so with the word; when you teach a child about God early on, they will be stronger in the faith as they grow up. This is not to say that they will be perfect and that they will not turn away. That is between them and God when they come of age. It is between you and God while they are young to instill the word.

When a matter is in a person's mind or thoughts, they will dwell on it until it begins to plague their heart. That is why it is imperative to plant seeds of love and Godliness in your children's minds first and foremost.

The bible says for as a man thinketh in his heart so is he. We want our children to have a solid foundation to build upon. Let us make sure that there is no room for corruption in the heart. Train their brain is a school adage that applies here also. It is not okay to just let anyone speak into your children's lives because not everyone knows how to speak life or choose to speak life.

That same way that we would protect our children from a child molester or murderer, we need to protect them from people who plant discord and wicked thoughts into their young minds.

Children are very vulnerable, and their hearts are easily taken and open to much.

I can recall my heart literally breaking simply because another child did not want to play with me. I had not been trained in my brain to understand that it was of no fault of my own, so I took that to heart. I took that as though something was wrong with me, and that thought set up residence in my heart, and it garnered how I dealt with friendships and relationships from that point on. I was very guarded and untrusting.

Even now, as an adult, almost thirty-five years later, I deal with rejection and trust issues, even when there is clearly no need for my guard to be in place.

I recall a little girl, no more than three, who was telling her mother that her heart hurt.

The mom thought this was a cute scene and recorded the child saying it, but the child was literally in tears. Something was wrong. Something had hurt this baby deeply, and her heart was truly hurt. The mother could not see past the cuteness of the little girl's face.

We have to be ever so careful to listen to our children, to pay close attention to what they say. We cannot discount their feelings because they are children. Who knows what that little girl was crying and upset about.

That is how the enemy comes in and steals our children right from under us. They come to us and tell us that their hearts are hurting, that they need us, that they need to talk, and we shut them down, saying, what do you have to be worried about; go play. We tend to think that as children, they do not face anything and that nothing hurts their hearts. Just because they are young and tend to forgive easily does not mean that their hearts aren't hurting. Listen to your children, listen to their hearts. Help them fill their hearts with Jesus so that no evil thoughts can overtake them.

I am a living testimony to the detriment that can be done to a child's heart by mere words alone. As parents, let us speak life to our children and guard their hearts. They are precious gifts given to us to take care of, love, and cherish until God calls them back to Him.

We are not only to cover them in prayer for their physical protection, but we are also to pray for them in spirit as we know the enemy seeks to destroy them at the very essence of themselves.

That being said, I want every parent to join me in praying for our children's hearts to be guarded by The Lord Jesus Christ. The Lord should be the center of their hearts. Let us pray that HE becomes that for our seed. It is so imperative for them to live, flourish, and be victorious over the enemy.

Prayer: Their Hearts

Oh, Precious Father God, I ask that you will be the center of our children's hearts. Lord come in and fill_____________________ with your love and your compassion. Show up in them and live in them. God, abide in them daily so that the enemy will take a second guess before even approaching them.

God let there be a shield around their hearts that will guard them against the lies and plots of the enemy. I pray that you will take up space therein and not allow the enemy any place in which to dwell.

Father, I pray that above all, they will seek to honor you in their hearts. I want them to be so filled with your love that their hearts will pour out in abundance just who you are.

God, I realize that if they have you living on the inside of them, no devil in hell can touch them. Though he may bring trials and issues to their flesh, you will guard their spirit as long as you live in their hearts. I thank you for being the heart of my children every day. I give you glory, and I receive it now that they are blessed beyond measure and that you and you alone guard their hearts. They have on your full armor, and not only

are they protected, but they are
victorious.

Chapter Four

Their Souls

I want you to know that in all the praying over the mind and heart that we do, our children's souls are the most important thing to pray for. It is that which the enemy seeks to take possession of at all costs. In the beginning, he may have a hard time swaying the mind and the heart, but he knows that if he keeps on pulling and pressing, he will wear down someone who is not entirely rooted and grounded in the Lord. The bible tells us to watch, fight and pray. If we allow ourselves to get lax in any area, we leave ourselves open to the enemy's attacks on our minds and hearts. When we do that, the soul is now at stake. We have to be sure and cover our children's souls.

We have to pray that the enemy does not take possession of them in that manner.

It is also important to realize how he does that. Satan is crafty, and he knows that we are on the lookout for the obvious things that he can and will do to trip us up, bind us and make us miss the mark. We are ready for those situations, problems, and trials because we expect them to come.

We, as parents, are quick to pray that our children do not get caught up in drugs, gangs, or violence. However, we do not think along lines that go deeper than that. We fail to realize, especially in this day and age, that children have a lot more going on in their lives. They are being faced with some serious issues.

I can recall my biggest problem at nine years old was that I didn't get the doll I wanted for Christmas. Now, nine-year-olds deal with being molested or having their youth taken away by someone selling them for sex. We have to be honest with ourselves and know that the enemy is playing for keeps, and he wants our children's souls. It is no longer enough to teach our children the simple bedtime prayer: Now I lay down to sleep I pray the Lord my soul to keep; if I should die before I wake, I pray that Lord my soul to take. No, we have to start early and go deep. We must implant soul-saving prayers and words of prayer into our children. Just as the Lord calls the young because they are strong, so does satan want them for the very same reason. He wants to build him up an army of soldiers just as God does. He wants to infect them with lies, hatred, malice, and pure evil. He is after the souls of our children.

How can we fight against his attacks? How can we make sure that our children's souls are saved?

First of all, we as parents have to stop seeing our children as babies who do not need to know the Bible's truth. Too often, we feel that our prayers are enough to shield them. It is vital that we do pray for our children, but at the same time, some of our children are more anointed than we are. We cannot keep holding them back or making them be silent when they want to know more about the bible and when they want to speak on something. The bible says to us clearly in Matthew 19:14, "Let the children come to me and do not hinder them for to such belongs the kingdom of heaven." God knows what He is doing, and He knows far better than we do how to shield and cover and prepare and care for and equip us, as well as our children. Sometimes we get in the way, and we need to move back and let God do what He wants to do through them. Your very own salvation may come through your child. So, teach them the word and be teachable, for you never know who God is using. So, that being said, tell the gospel truth that hell is real and that eternity is forever. If they do not live a holy life, that their eternity will be spent in torment. There is a way to break it down on a level where they understand it and fear God, but not be afraid of God. We have to learn the ins and outs, which come through prayer and opening our hearts to help.

The next thing that we need to do is trust the process. This book is all about cutting the cord and letting go.

I was a witness to some children who attended church, and their guardian would not allow the children to interact with the other children or the youth teachers and leaders. They would have to sit out in front with all the seasoned saints and listen to lessons that they cannot relate to or could not understand. They seemed bored and disconnected. The guardian did not realize that she was hurting the children instead of helping them. In her eyes, she was protecting their souls from wrong teachings based on others' opinions. It was as if no one knew the word of God as well as them, and they were the only true Christians. We have to learn to cut the cord and understand that as much as we love our children and as much as we want them to know the word of God that it may not be through us that they get every aspect. I know for my children that they will talk to others about things that they do not feel comfortable talking to me about. These were men and women of God who were teaching my children the right way to live and respond to the issues they were having. I had to understand that God can and will use whom He chooses. We are not the only connection to God that our children have, though we should be the first and always be there for them. Had I refused to allow my children to have these Godly relationships and interact with their Sunday School Teachers and youth leaders, I would be hindering growth to their soul.

If they could not release their fears, anxiety, anger, and feelings to someone, it could negatively affect them, and who knows how the enemy would use it against them.

We know that it is his will to destroy them, and he means by any means, killing the soul being his primary goal.

So, we have to learn to allow our children to have other Godly role models and teachers in their lives to guide them because their souls are at stake. Let us not hinder them, but help them.

Another way to ensure that our children's souls are anchored in the Lord is to live a saved life before them. We can pray all day but if we are not living a sanctified life before them, then what they see is what they sow. We have to live a saved life and show and prove how crucial it is to have our soul anchored in The Lord.

Children see what you do before they hear what you say. In all your doing, do it right. Do not just teach and preach the word but live it.

We have to be careful to pour and speak life into our children. What we do and say to them creates soul ties.

Soul ties are usually spoken of as when someone has an intimate relationship with another, and their spirits connect. However, this is not only deemed in the sense of sexual. What closer bond of intimacy is there than that of a mother and child. There is a bond there. You are the first person to hold that child, love them, shape, and mold them. You are a part of them.

We too often speak damning things on our children, not even realizing it. I know that coming from a black family who was just very direct, we talk rough. It is not that we do not love one another; we are just straightforward and rough. I think that it was a way of making us tough, teaching us how to survive in a cold, cruel world. If we fell, we were not pampered; it was like, "Girl, you better get your butt up and go on somewhere and play." If we said we were depressed, it was like, "If you do not shut that mess up!" This was just how it was. Was it love? Maybe. Did it leave scars? Did it create soul ties? Definitely. So, things that we do or say out of habit or in just can really be detrimental and really affect not only our children's feelings but their hearts and souls as well. This may have been how we were raised, and perhaps it is a cycle that needs to be broken in us. So, let us go to God in prayer for our children and our own soul. In order to break soul ties, we must first

understand and admit that they
exist. So, let us go to God in prayer.

Prayer: Their Souls

Heavenly Father, please help me and my children not be laden with the past's soul ties. Help me recognize any soul ties that have me bound so that I can break them and not push them onto my children.

God, please forgive me for the times that I have put the burden of such ties on my children. God, I'm asking that you set me free from soul ties so that I can pray such things off my children. I release any excuses that allowed me to think it was okay to place such heaviness on my child's soul. I repent of the very thought of it being okay to say whatever I wanted because they are just children, after all. Father, I take full responsibility for accepting the load of soul ties, and now I give that burden to you. My child and myself, we leave them at your feet. We are free because your son Jesus Christ came to set us free, and whom the Son sets free is free indeed. Father, I thank you for being a great God who can handle all the ties and weights we once bared. I speak in past tense because it is finished. In Jesus' name, our soul has been set free, and it is so. Amen.

Chapter Five

Their Growth

It is a beautiful thing and a hard thing for a parent to see their child growing up. We love it, yet we fear it. It is the time when we are most proud and most afraid. It is when we realize that they are no longer in our lap but sit heavily on our hearts. These days it is no longer when they turn eighteen and graduate from high school. Children are growing up so much faster now, and they want their freedom so much sooner. How do we as parents cope with letting go? The only answer I have for that one is prayer. I can honestly tell you that this is yet a struggle for me, which is why God gave me this book. Every single chapter is hitting me, and I mean hard. These are no love taps. As I sit and write, I feel each lick with force. Hey, you all just gone have to do like me and take it like a soldier.

There is no place in God for fear and heavy hearts. We have to let go of those thoughts and know that no matter how much our kids grow up, they are never entirely on their own. Though they may not be looking to us for all the answers, we can be assured if we have trained them

It is our duty to release them and let them go. This is the difficult part; this is where obedience in us has to show forth. We teach our children the importance of obeying us as mothers and fathers, and now it is time for us to take that same sound advice and obey our Father.

I have a son who is seventeen. He thinks like a full-grown man always has been well ahead of his time. I have a middle daughter who is twenty-one, and she is our "Old Soul." My oldest daughter has been a mature young lady for so many of her twenty-four years that she seems much older. They all have a natural sense of wisdom, and I see it. I know that they just get a life and understand things differently from their peers. You would think that would give me great ease of mind in allowing them to step out into the world and be their own person and live their own lives to the fullest, but each of them will tell you that is not the case.

When I was a child and young adult as well, I was so sheltered by my mother that I made a vow never to treat my children in that manner. I said when I have kids, I'm going to let them have fun, go places, date, and live their own lives. I was so sure that my mother was smothering me. Now, I realize that it was just her way of loving me and trying to protect me. On the same note, I also realize how it stunted me in many areas of my life. There were some things that God wanted to do through me early on, but because she was holding onto me so tightly and refusing to cut the cord, I couldn't be released to work in my purpose fully.

I recall a situation where I was a teenager, and I went to a tent revival. This was an outdoor church service. My mother allowed me to go, but then she showed up. When I tell you the enemy is strategic in his plotting, you better believe it. The moment she showed up, I was high in The Spirit. I had caught the Holy Ghost and was having myself a time in The Lord.

About four women were ushers who surrounded me to make sure that I did not fall or bump into anyone or anything. These were women who were used to going to church and knew what it was for the Spirit to be moving. Though I knew as well, my mother did not. She saw the women as holding me hostage in the circle and not allowing me to leave. She felt that there was something wrong, and she wanted everything in her to protect her child. The next thing any of them knew, she had pulled out a knife and was threatening all of them. She told them to let me go. I am oblivious to all of this because I praise God and seek to breakthrough and break free. Way back then, God knew who and what I was going to be in Him…so did satan. This was such a sad, and I must say, embarrassing occurrence. For a long time after that, I was left questioning the ushers, the pastors, and the evangelists. I was confused about what was right and what was wrong. I couldn't understand why my mother would be so angry if they were only trying to help me. The thing is, my mother didn't understand that it was helpful. This goes back to breaking free from the past and asking God to help you before you can be any help at all to your children. If you do not do so, you too will be hurt and a hindrance to them and their growth.

God wanted to do something exceptional and mind-blowing through me on that night, and I feel if He had that, even my mother and more of my household could have come into the knowledge of Him and gotten saved.

We have to stop leaning on our own understanding because we do not know the/ plans God has for our children's lives, and we end up stunting their growth and delaying their destiny.

There are many heartaches that I went through that I know I could have avoided had my growth in Christ not been stunted by unbelief and ignorance of God's word and plan.

At the same time, I fully understand and know that it all worked out for my good. Those trials taught me lessons and built my character. They showed me the error of my ways and how not to parent. The thing is, I only got this revelation recently.

I said with the fruit of my lips that I would not stunt my children's growth, yet that was precisely what I was doing. I am learning to let go. I am learning to cut the cord, and now I can unleash my prayers.

My oldest daughter has a baby, and she is a first-time mom. I see so many things I would not do or do, but I do better because I know better now. The moment I tell her how to do it, she will buck against me and do it even more so the way she sees fit. I have to cut the cord and let her raise her baby on her own. All I can do as a grandmother is to love, spoil and unleash my prayers. If I am constantly arguing with my daughter, then I'm not praying. We both want what is best for my grandbaby; that could be one thing to me and a totally different thing for her. God knows what's best, and He knows how to get the best out of all of us. Therefore, if I take it to Him, all is going to be well. My grandbaby will be blessed, I'm going to be happy, and my daughter will experience growth.

Will there be growing pains along the way? Yes, for both of us. Still, it is growth for both of us.

The next prayer is for growth, for parents and children.

Prayer: Their Growth

Dear Most Gracious and Heavenly Father, I come before you as humbly as I know, asking that you would pivot my child into a spiritual growth spurt that would elevate them beyond any evil in this world. By that, I mean that even though they face trials and challenging tasks, the growth that has come upon them will unleash a power like none the enemy can handle. They will no longer fall in the same pits that they once were enslaved to. They will have a new sense of who they are in you. My children will be able to withstand any firey trial and hold their heads high in integrity and walk in grace. No longer will they argue and debate over what is right, for your commandments will be embedded in their minds and at the forefront of their hearts. God, I trust you to grow my children up in you, and in making this declaration, I too will grow.

I will no longer hold onto my children as if they will be lost without me. I will live as if I understand that it is in you that they live, move, and have their being. I will release them to you and keep them covered in prayer. This will begin to show you a growth in me that I can unleash every prayer. God, I trust you with my life; therefore, I must trust you with my children. I am claiming victory in the area of growth

for myself and my children. And it is
so. In Jesus mighty precious name,
Amen.

Chapter Six

Their Lifestyle

As parents, we often look at our adult children's lifestyle, and we cringe. We tend to think that we have somehow failed as a parent; it all does not meet our standards.

Say, for instance, you raised your children in church, and you taught them the word of God, and you lived it to the best of your ability. You were that true light, and you showed them the correct path according to the bible, yet they still stray. Your daughter is promiscuous; your son is on drugs, your other son is in a gang, your other daughter is in prison. What in the world happened? Where did you go wrong? Are these really my children? The children I raised? The children I prayed for? The children I stayed on my face before God for?

Well, let me help you out here. You did not go wrong. The world happened. It always does. We are saved. We are not of the world, but we do live in the world, and sometimes no matter how hard we try, we fall. So, how is it so impossible to think that our children cannot fall as well? We have to stop putting a sign on our heads that read Perfect Parents. There is no such thing, and the higher you set your standards as such, the harder you will fall when your children choose to walk their own path.

It does not mean that you have failed as a parent, that you did not raise your children to be righteous, that you did pray for them, that you did not stay on your face before God for them. It simply means that God gives everyone free will, and just as He does not force anyone to serve Him and live a holy life, neither can we force such upon anyone, not even our children. All we can do is raise them right, train them up.

Ultimately, they have to make a choice to serve God on their own.

Often they choose a totally different lifestyle. That is because they belong to you, and if the enemy cannot get to you, he will go through them to try that much harder. Let's be clear that satan is no fool; he knows where a mother's heart lies; with her children, her babies.

Often, your children do not even understand why they choose to live the type of lifestyle they live. Evil spirits have overcome them.

If you ask someone why they are on drugs, they will not say it is because they want to. They are just not able to get off.

How many people do you know would continue harming themselves and enjoying it or want to continue on that path? Every person I've met who has been on drugs has wanted to get off, they wanted better for themselves, but an evil spirit controlled them.

We have to know to pray for our adult children and not judge them or argue with them. This only opens the door to worse behavior and them potentially cutting us off completely. Also, we have to know how to pray for them. We cannot go to God for our children in an accusatory manner. When we go in that spirit, we are not in a place where God will answer our prayers. We have to understand who the true enemy is and fight him in prayer the right way.

Being completely honest with ourselves, we can recall a time where our lifestyle was not

that of a Christian, and we were doing some things that we now see as revolting or disgusting. There were certain behaviors that we exhibited that were the exact opposite of anything Christlike. So, just because we have given our hearts to The Lord, we have no room to judge. We were once lost, and it was not us but the Spirit dwelling in us that caused us to sin. Our children have that same sinful nature, and we have to exercise compassion when we pray, remembering it is not our children who are acting out or trying to hurt us; it is the spirit that is possessing them. Once we learn to deal with the real problem and principality, we will know how to attack it.

So, let's pray that the spirits of evil be broken off our children's lives instead of praying against our children themselves.

Prayer: Their Lifestyle

Heavenly Father, I come before you now asking that you clear my mind of any judgment against my child/children. I know that it is not their desire to sin and to hurt themselves. I see the enemy at work in their lives, and I am asking that you allow them to see him as well. I pray for shaking in their spirit.

God, I have raised my children to love, serve, and honor you. I know that they are given free will. I am not trying to force anything on them, but I am asking that you touch their hearts to bring about a change. I pray that you would get to the root of the sin in their life. I ask that you would draw them to you. Father, every word instilled in them according to your commandments, bring it back to their remembrance and lets it spark a do right spirit within them.

God, we know that all things are subject to you. Satan is the ruler of the dark world, but You even have control over him. As a mother, I am unleashing my prayer to you for my children's minds. I am praying that they return to you and live a holiness lifestyle and not hell. No matter what demons they face, greater is He who is in me than he who is in the world.

I receive that my children will live prosperous and holy lives in the name of The Lord Jesus. Amen.

Chapter Seven

Their Turnaround

As we pray for our children, we do not always see immediate results, but we must remain faithful that God is working in their lives. That He is working the situation out for their good. There are times when God tells us to do something, and we tend to want to take our time in doing it, yet we want Him to be very punctual with our prayers.

We have to know that sometimes even in the waiting, God is doing great things. If He were to answer our prayers immediately, where would that leave us? Cocky and confident to the point that everything we want our children to do, we just run and tell God.

No, it should not be so. We want God to break our children. In His working things out, there will have to be some hurt, some growing pains, some pruning, and some hardness. The fire is not to burn them but to build them into the glorious diamond that God wants them to be, not what we want them to be.

If I push and push for God to send my daughter or son to a place of elevation that they have not been properly pruned for, they will only fall from grace again. We need to learn to allow God to work in them and do complete work in them. It is not up to us when they come off the potters' wheel. We are not that potter; God is. He knows exactly what He is doing, and He does not need our help to accomplish it.

A finished work by God is complete, and there is no room left for any failure.

Once we learn just to let go, cut the cord, and allow God to work in His own time, then all will be well.

Looking back on the prodigal son's story, it was not the next day that the son came back home. The father had to wait some time for his son to come to himself and return home.

The son had to go through some things; he had to reach his absolute rock bottom before returning to himself and realizing that all he had to do is go home.

We have to allow those rock bottom experiences in our children's lives. They do not feel good or look good, but we have to allow them. God has to show our children themselves. We as parents can talk until we are blue in the face, but only God can bring deliverance and a genuine turnaround.

If we just pray and wait on God, we will begin to see a turnaround. There is nothing too hard for God. That drug abuser can be delivered, that wayward child can turn around, that prodigal son can return home. You just pray and wait on God. In that waiting, prepare a feast for your child is coming home. God will not fail. The turnaround is coming.

Prayer: Their Turnaround

Father God, I see that in all things, you are God. I am not going to look at the state that my child has come to live in. I will think about the way I raised them. I will focus on the word that I know is within them; I will trust you to work the process of a turnaround in them.

I understand that my timing is not your timing and that you are preparing an excellent turnaround for them. No matter what it looks like, I know that you can turn it around. I know that you can bring deliverance. I know that you are a mighty and powerful God.

I trust you to be in complete control, and I know that you have not forgotten about my child, and I know that you hear my prayers. There is no stronghold that the enemy has on my child that you cannot break. Thank You, God, for the turnaround. I receive it in Jesus' name.

Chapter Eight

Their Future

God knows the future that He has planned for our children, and we need to look through heaven's eyes and see that same future. We need to learn to declare and decree a great destiny over our children.

In the natural we want our children to have a great future; therefore, we sow into them. We make sure that they do their homework, that they are at school every day if at all possible, that they are doing their homework, that they are doing their very best, that they graduate, that they go to college, that they date, and marry the right person for them.

So, spiritually we need to invest in their future as well. No matter what it may be looking like in the present tense, we have to believe in God for our children's great future.

When I was only a child, I began reading the bible, writing bible stories, poems, and other stories. God already knew then the future that He had planned for me. My mother did not know the plans of God, for she was not saved.

This was somewhat a delay in the promise of my future being fulfilled, but look at God; it is so. Nothing can stop the plan and promise of God in our lives, in our children's lives. Just think of how much greater of an impact you can have by sowing into that future from day one living and believing in the promises of God.

Even if you have neglected to do so as your children were growing up, you can still pray over your adult children's future. It is not too late to see the promises of God manifest in their lives.

Too often, we get caught up in what is going on right in front of us. I do not believe that John-John has a bright future because he is stealing and cursing others today. I cannot see Sally-Mae doing great things for the Lord because all she does is lie and persecute the church. This is what the enemy wants us to focus on; the situation and not ever get the true revelation of what God will do.

We have to break these cycles and trust God to do abundantly above all we could think or ask. We have to trust that if God said it, it shall come to pass. We have to learn to speak life no matter what it looks like. We cannot always jump in and tell our children to get it right; we just need to trust God that they will. He holds their future in His hands, and the sooner we cut the cord that we have on them and allow God to deal with them, the sooner they can secure a promising future in Christ. We know that God only wants the best for our children, but how He goes about giving that to them is totally up to Him. Just relax and watch God Be God.

Prayer: Their Future

Dear God, I know that you hold my child's future in your hands; therefore, I take off the limits that I place on them by trying to take control. I cannot fix, change, or redirect any path you have laid before them. It is not up to me to set their destiny. You have already done just that. I pray that you will give my children a future of hope, success, and, most importantly, everlasting life in you. Please help me to trust the process and help me to not look at the here and now. I know you are able; I know you are in control; I know you created them; I know you made all things; I know you are the Alpha and

Omega; I know you are the beginning and the end. I trust you, God, to be God of their here, now, and their future. Thank you, God, that their future entails heaven as their final destination and that I have peace in knowing this fact. In Jesus' name, I thank you, and I praise you. Amen.

Chapter Nine

It is Finished

I love these famous last words of Jesus before He died on the cross for our sins.

This solidified all things. It is finished. This tells me that when doubt tries to creep in that, I have not done my best in raising my children, I can tell doubt to go. Why? Because It is finished.

This tells me that when hopelessness tries to overwhelm me when I think my kids will not ever get it right, I can let that spirit know that it is a lie. Why? Because It is finished.

Those words from Jesus tell me that when I feel like all the time I poured into releasing this book, which God gave me word for word was in vain, I can say not so. Why? Because It is finished.

This book is more than just a book of prayers to help mothers, fathers, guardians release their children and let God have them. This book is a testament to what God can do. I am an author, and I have written many books, but this one was done in a matter of days, and each time I sat at the computer keyboard, God guided my thoughts and mind. I never had to think about what to type next. I just allowed God to take control of my thoughts and move my fingers. I do not think I have ever typed so fast or with such an anointing. This book is going to reach many and help several. God never sends His word out, and it returns void. So, this book is not just a book; it is a miracle. It is God at work. It is God showing up and proving just who He is and just what He can do.

So, if you are reading this book, whether you purchased it, received it as a gift, or even borrowed it from someone. I want you to get that it was placed in your hands for a reason. I want you to know that if you were that child who was told you were not good enough. It is finished. You are good enough. You always were good enough.

Suppose you are that mom who struggles to see the good in yourself, to see that you may not always get it right, but that God yet loves you. You are loved. You are doing your best, and you are not alone. Be proud that you stuck it out, and know that God has greater plans for you.

I never want you to allow or give the enemy a place to make you feel that your efforts are not enough.

They are. I never want you to feel that your gifts are not appreciated. They are. I never want you to feel that your work is inadequate and not providing enough; it is. I never want you to allow satan to make you feel your child would have been better off with someone else. That is a lie. God makes no mistakes. If He allowed you to have a child, to raise a child, to love a child, then it was meant for you to do these things. You are not beneath; you are above. You are not the tail; you are the head. You are not to listen to and believe the lies of the enemy any longer. You are enough. Put the devil in his place and tell him It is finished.

If you are that father who was never given a chance due to bitterness or resentment, there is always hope. God can mend and reconcile. Do not give up. Hope is a powerful weapon; just make sure faith is its partner. God can and will make it right.

You do not have to accept the title of a deadbeat dad. You do not have to allow people to put such labels on you, and you just roll with it. If you want to be that amazing father to your child, then do it.

Pray and ask God to guide you on how and when to take the steps toward doing that. You deserve it, and your child deserves it. This book is for mothers and fathers alike, so cut the cord of bitterness, anger, and resentment. Set the record straight by fighting in prayer and watch those prayers be unleashed for you. God has no respect for persons. Mothers and fathers alike are deserving of a healthy relationship with their children that extends into them having a great relationship with Christ.

If you are a guardian who did not first choose to be a parent but were just thrown into it, know that it was your destiny. Know that you are changing, shaping, molding, and influencing the life or lives of some incredible and unique children entrusted to you by God. It was not by accident; it was on purpose, for a purpose. Trust God that He makes no mistakes, and though you might, He is still right there with you. You have got this. Keep pushing. You may not have given birth to the child, but God is giving you the opportunity to birth some amazing Godly characteristics and qualities into them.

Do not ever let the enemy make you feel like you are not that child's parent and that they cannot mimic your lifestyle and be your child, because they are your child. Keep instilling virtue and values in them, and keep watching God unleash your powerful prayers.

For the parents whose children are now grown. Please, parents, do not force your thoughts, opinions, and feelings on them; cut the cord and unleash your prayers. Trust that you have done a great job raising them and knowing that every single moral and value you taught them is within. Even more so, know that every word of life, liberty, hope, trust, faith, love, joy, goodness, hope, prosperity, peace, and salvation; every word of God that you poured into them will come to the forefront of their heart and they will live it and pass it on to their seed as you did to them.

You have to understand that even in your slackness and your mistakes that God was building them up. We were not meant to be there to cushion every fall, kiss every boo-boo, and heal every broken heart. If we are the heroes in their lives, what does that leave room for them to trust God?

We have to know that as they grew up, God was growing us up as well. Come on, Mother, you did it!!! You made it!!! They made it!!! Cut the cord, and let God do the rest.

Forgive yourself for any and every feeling of inadequacy. Why? Because It is finished.

Love and Blessings

Marilyn Kay Brooks Simmons

Final Thoughts

I cannot close this book out without saying that I had the best mother for me.

I thank God for every moment spent with the beautiful and loving, caring, and wonderful Lynell (Laura Nell) Brooks.

She did the very best that she could with what she was given. I learned so much from her, and even though she is no longer alive, she is yet teaching me how to be a better mother with all the fond and funny memories I shared with her. I thank God for a mother like her who loved me despite disobedience and flaws. She was indeed the best Mama ever to my siblings and me.

Nells Baby

Her children arise up and call her blessed; and her husband (also), and he praiseth her.
Proverbs 31:28

Let's Connect

Email: marilynsimmons90@yahoo.com
Social media: @marilynsimmons_official